Mr. Digby's Bad Day

By Jerry Smath & Valerie Smath • Illustrated by Jerry Smath

Simon and Schuster Books for Young Readers

PUBLISHED BY SIMON & SCHUSTER INC., NEW YORK

SIMON AND SCHUSTER BOOKS FOR YOUNG READERS
Simon & Schuster Building, Rockefeller Center
1230 Avenue of the Americas, New York, New York 10020

SIMON AND SCHUSTER BOOKS FOR YOUNG READERS
is a trademark of Simon & Schuster Inc.
Manufactured in the United States of America

10 9 8 7 6 5 4 3 2 1

Library of Congress Cataloging-in-Publication Data
Smath, Jerry.   Mr. Digby's bad day
by Jerry Smath and Valerie Smath.
Summary: When Mr. Digby takes a walk through town,
his umbrella will not stay shut and he unknowingly causes
several minor accidents.
[1. Umbrellas and parasols—Fiction.]   I. Smath, Valerie.
II. Title.   88-29856
PZ7.S6393Mr   1989   CIP
[E]—dc19   AC
ISBN 0-671-67802-7

To
Martha, Ethel, Theresa, Betty, and Ruth
—very special ladies.

J.S. & V.S.

Mr. Digby woke up from a sound sleep. It had rained the night before, but now the sun was shining.

He opened the window and took a deep breath of fresh air.

"What a wonderful day for a walk," he said.

He put on his best walking coat and top hat.

Mr. Digby always believed in dressing well.

"My, but you are a handsome fellow," he said, looking in the hall mirror.

Mr. Digby put his umbrella over his arm and started down the steps.

He saw his neighbor, Mrs. Wiggleton, coming down the street with her pet.

"Good morning, dear lady," said Mr. Digby with a courtly bow.

Mr. Digby always believed in being polite.

"You won't need your umbrella today," said Mrs. Wiggleton, "it's not raining."

"One can never tell," said Mr. Digby, "and I always believe in being prepared."

But then, as he turned to walk away, his umbrella
popped open.

Mrs. Wiggleton jumped with surprise, and her pet
went flying through the air.

Mr. Digby never saw what had happened
to Mrs. Wiggleton and her pet. He only noticed that
his umbrella had opened.

"Silly umbrella," he said, as he snapped it shut.

When he got to the corner, Mr. Digby stopped to buy
a flower from the flower lady. He paid for the flower
and put it in his lapel.

Mr. Digby always believed in looking smart.

But then, while he admired himself in a store window, his umbrella popped open again. It bumped a peddler's cart and sent it bouncing into the street.

Fruits and vegetables rolled everywhere. People slipped on bananas, tripped over watermelons, and sat, with splats, on tomatoes.

Mr. Digby was not aware of what had happened.
He was only aware that his umbrella had opened again.
"Troublesome thing," he said, as he snapped it shut
and walked on.

Mr. Digby passed his favorite restaurant. The smell
of food made him hungry, so he decided to stop.

    While Mr. Digby was eating his lunch, a stray dog sat looking at him. He knew the dog was hungry.

    "Don't worry little doggie," said Mr. Digby. "I'll save you some of my food."

    Mr. Digby always believed in being kind to animals.

When he finished eating, he kept his promise. He paid
for his lunch and asked the waiter to put some food
in a bag for the dog.

But when Mr. Digby bent over to feed the dog...
guess what?

But Mr. Digby never noticed the trouble his umbrella had caused. He only noticed that it had opened again.

"Foolish umbrella," he said, as he snapped it shut and kept walking.

It happened again!

Mr. Digby's umbrella popped open, knocking a tray of food out of a waiter's hands.

Dishes and food went flying everywhere, and on everyone. Soon hungry, barking dogs came running from all over the neighborhood.

Mr. Digby was far from home when suddenly it began to rain.

"It's a good thing I'm always prepared," said Mr. Digby, as he started to open his umbrella.

It wouldn't budge. He tried again and again, but it was stuck shut.

So Mr. Digby started to walk home.

As he walked, his umbrella was getting fatter and fatter
as it filled with rainwater. But he didn't notice.

Then Mr. Digby saw a trolley coming down the street.
He ran as fast as he could and got on.

The trolley was very crowded. Mr. Digby had just sat down when the conductor came by to collect the fare.

Mr. Digby reached for his wallet. It was empty… and so were his pockets!

"I'm afraid I have no money left," he said. "I have spent it all."

The conductor became angry. "If you wish to ride this trolley," he said, "you must be prepared to pay."

"But I am always prepared," cried Mr. Digby.

However, this time Mr. Digby was not prepared,
and he was told to leave.

But as he stepped off the trolley his umbrella burst
open again, splashing all the people with water.

Then the doors slammed shut.

Inside the trolley people were wet and angry. "Come on, let's get going!" they screamed. "We want to go home!"

Outside the trolley Mr. Digby pulled and pulled
on his umbrella, but it was no use. The door was stuck,
and finally he had to let go.

The trolley drove off, leaving Mr. Digby standing
in the rain without his umbrella.

He was feeling quite alone when the stray dog
he had fed came up to him.

"You can't stay outside in this awful weather,"
said Mr. Digby. "You will come home with me."
He scooped up the dog and put him inside his coat.

There was nothing more he could do now but walk
home, and that was what he did.

Just as they reached the house it stopped raining and the sun came out. Mr. Digby and his new friend walked up the steps.

"Today was a bad day," he said, "but tomorrow will be better."

Mr. Digby always believed in better tomorrows.